10-9

Sing, Sophie!

Dayle Ann Dodds

illustrated by Rosanne Litzinger

CANDLEWICK PRESS
CAMBRIDGE, MASSACHUSETTS

Little Sophie Adams had a voice so big folks claimed they could hear her from Corn County clear to the Oklahoma border.

"I *loooooove* to sing!" said Sophie, strumming her guitar.

My dog ran off, my cat has fleas,
My fish won't swim, and I hate peas.
But I'm a cowgirl through and through,
Yippee-ky-yee!
Yippee-ky-yuu!

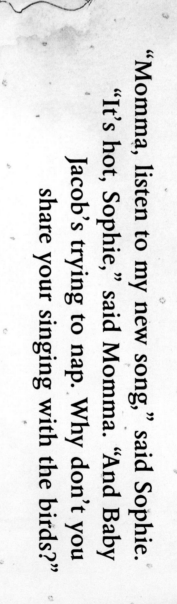

"Momma, listen to my new song," said Sophie.

"It's hot, Sophie," said Momma. "And Baby Jacob's trying to nap. Why don't you share your singing with the birds?"

"Aw, Momma." Sophie took her voice out into the garden. She strummed her guitar and sang out her song:

My rooster won't crow, my hen won't lay.

My frog got warts and hopped away.

My legs are skinny,

my toes are fat.

I've got the temper of a tiger cat.
But I'm a cowgirl, don't you know!
Yippee–ky–yee! Yippee–ky–yo!

"Sophie! You stop that bellowing right now!" Sophie's older sister, Kate-Ellen, called. "With this sticky heat and all your racket, my new fluffy hairdo is fixin' to fall flat as a flapjack!"

"Oh, fiddle-faddle," mumbled Sophie. "Doesn't anyone want to hear my new song?"

At the creek she flopped down under a shady sassafras tree. Once again, Sophie began strumming and singing:

My coat is torn,
my shoes are wet,
My socks don't match,
my rat's upset.
My kite got stuck.
I ate a bug.
I spilled red cider
on the rug.

But I'm a cowgirl
tried and true,
Yippee-ky-yee!
Yippee-ky-yuu!

"For Pete's sake,
Sophie," said brother Willy.
"Can't you see I'm trying to fish?
Your caterwauling is scaring all the
fish away! Go somewhere else."

"Oh, chicken feathers!" Sophie said. "I've got a song in my heart and it needs to come out!"

Sophie leaned against the cool wall of the barn and strummed out a tune:

My jokes are bad,
my riddles no good.
My hair never curls
the way that it should.

But I'm a cowgirl, yessirree! Yippee-ky-yo! Yippee-ky-yee!

"Take your singing somewhere else, sweet pea," Sophie's pa called. "Old Betsy's getting fidgety in this heat and the milk pail's sitting empty."

"Oh, goose grease," said Sophie.
"Doesn't anyone want to hear me sing?"

She dragged her guitar out to the field
and sang to the corn and the crickets
until the sun went down.

That night a
summer storm hit.
FLASH! went the lightning.
BOOM! BOOM!
sounded the thunder.
Baby Jacob began to cry.

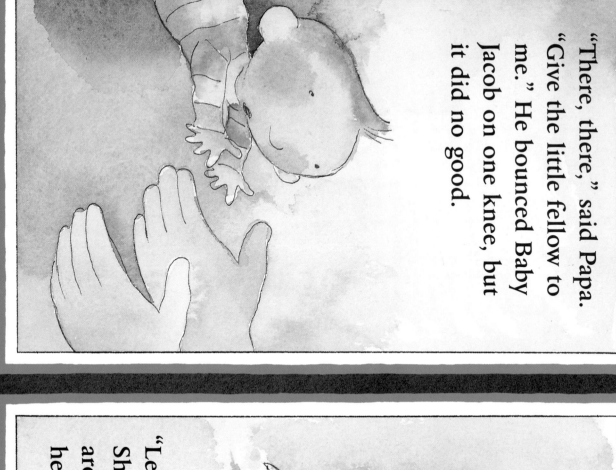

"There, there," said Papa. "Give the little fellow to me." He bounced Baby Jacob on one knee, but it did no good.

"Let me try," said Kate-Ellen. She twirled Baby Jacob all around the living room, but he went on crying.

"I'll get him to stop,"
said Willy. He dangled
a wiggly rubber worm
in front of Baby Jacob's
nose, but Baby Jacob
cried louder than ever:
"*WAAAAA!*"

"I have an idea," Sophie said. She took Baby Jacob into her arms. "Don't worry, Jacob."

She sat him in a chair and said, "That storm may be scary, but I'm not afraid." From the bottom of her heart, a song sang out—louder than thunder, stronger than lightning:

I hate spinach!
I hate liver!
Last week I fell
into the river.
I bumped my knee,
I scratched my nose,
I lost my shoe, I tore my clothes.
Whenever trouble passes by,
I don't worry. I don't cry.

Yippee yippee-ky-yee!
'Cause I'm a cowgirl, don't you see?
I'm a cowgirl, don't you see?

Baby Jacob giggled and clapped.
"He's smiling!" said Momma.
"He likes your song," said Papa.
"What a catchy tune!"
said Kate-Ellen.
"Not bad!" added Willy.
"Will you sing another?"
they all asked.

"Well, jumping jackrabbits!" Sophie said, strumming her guitar with glee. "I thought you'd never ask!"

Ducks and geese, they make me sneeze,
I have freckles on my knees.
I like Jell-O, mosquitoes like me,
I fell out of the big oak tree.
My ears are big,
my head is small.
It doesn't bother me at all.
I don't care!
Don't you know?

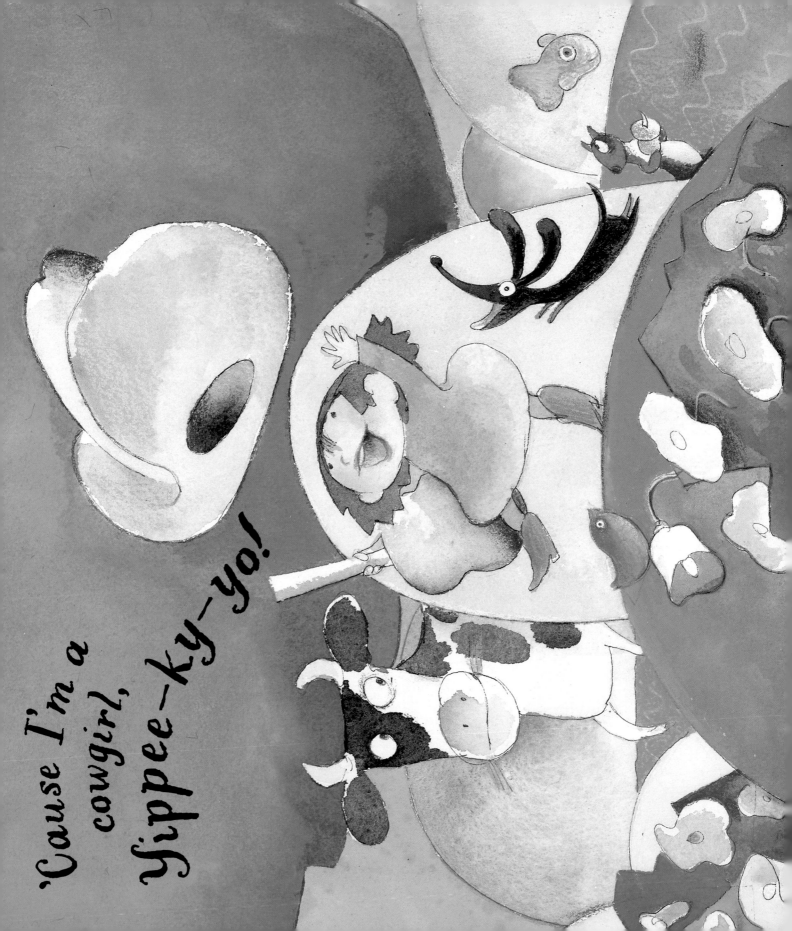

'Cause I'm a cowgirl, Yippee-ky-yo!

For Jaime, with a song in her heart
D.D.

To singing cowboys and cowgirls everywhere
R.L.

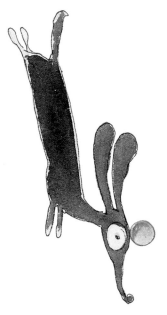

First U.S. paperback edition 1999

The Library of Congress has cataloged the hardcover edition as follows:

Dodds, Dayle Ann
Sing, Sophie! / Dayle Ann Dodds ; illustrated by Rosanne Litzinger.— 1st ed.
Summary: Although no one else in her family likes her loud voice,
Sophie's singing soothes her baby brother during a thunderstorm.
ISBN 0-7636-0131-4 (hardcover)
[1. Singing— Fiction. 2. Storms— Fiction.] I. Litzinger, Rosanne, ill. / II. Title.
PZ7.D6624Si   1997
[E]—dc20   96-22411

ISBN 0-7636-0500-X (paperback)

2 4 6 8 10 9 7 5 3 1

Printed in Hong Kong

This book was typeset in Columbus MT.
The illustrations were done in watercolor, gouache, and pencil.

Candlewick Press
2067 Massachusetts Avenue
Cambridge, Massachusetts 02140